I'M A BIG BROTHER

by Joanna Cole
Illustrated by Rosalinda Kightley

HARPER FESTIVAL

An Imprint of HarperCollinsPublishers

HarperFestival is an imprint of HarperCollins Publishers.

I'm a Big Brother
Text copyright © 1997 by Joanna Cole
Illustrations copyright © 2010 by Rosalinda Kightley
All rights reserved. Printed in the United States of America.
Library of Congress catalog card number: 2009927739
ISBN 978-0-06-190065-5

10 11 12 13 14   WOR   10 9 8 7 6 5 4 3 2 1
❖
Revised edition

Someone new is at our house.

Do you know who it is?

It's our baby!
I'm a big brother now!

The baby is so little.

Too little to walk.

Too little to talk.

Too little to play with toys.

Too little to eat pizza
or apples or ice cream.

Babies like to drink milk.

They like to sleep.

They like to be warm and cozy.

Our baby likes to look at me.

"Look at me, baby.
I'm your big brother."

Can I hold our baby?
I must ask Mommy first!

I am gentle with the baby.
I sing a little baby song.
I'm a big brother—I can make
our baby warm and cozy.

Sometimes the baby cries.
Daddy says, "Babies cry
to tell us something.
Let's see what's the matter."

Oh, it's time to change
the baby's diaper.
It's time for a bottle, too.
I can help—I'm a big brother now.

Mommy and Daddy show me pictures.
Pictures of me when I was a baby.
I was little, too—

just like our baby.

Now I am big! It's fun being big.
I can walk. I can talk.

I can play with toys.

I can eat pizza

and apples and ice cream!

Mommy loves me. Daddy loves me.
I am special to them.
I'm the only *me* in the whole world!

I'm special in a new way, too—
I'm a big brother now!

What a BIG BROTHER Needs

When there's a new baby in the house, an older sibling
needs a little extra—a little extra guidance, a little extra
reassurance, and a little extra love. Here are some ways
to help your older child adjust to his new role.

Be sure to set aside time just for your older child. Also, remember to be attentive to him in the presence of the baby, so he feels that he is an important member of the family. Even when you believe you're giving him more than ever, try to understand that it's natural for him to be demanding. Reassure him that your love for him hasn't changed.

Let him know that it's natural for a big brother to feel proud and loving and, at the same time, jealous and angry. Help him express his feelings but communicate clearly that it's not okay to *act* on negative feelings. And don't forget to praise him for good behavior, saying: "It's nice that you are being gentle" and "Thank you for getting the diaper. You're a big help!"

Explain that a newborn has different needs and limitations. That way your older child won't be too disappointed to discover that the baby can't play with him yet. At the same time, show him how the baby can respond to him, so he can begin forming a relationship.

Realize that you can't do everything perfectly all the time. Remember to give yourself a little extra attention, too. Watching the loving bond between your children grow will make up for those frustrating moments.

A caring family has plenty of love to go around!